It's So Nice to Have a Wolf Around the House

Story by Harry Allard   Pictures by James Marshall

A Picture Yearling Book

Published by
Bantam Doubleday Dell Books for Young Readers
a division of
Bantam Doubleday Dell Publishing Group, Inc.
1540 Broadway
New York, New York 10036

The trademarks Yearling® and Dell® are registered
in the U.S. Patent and Trademark Office and in other countries.
ISBN: 0-440-41353-2
Reprinted by arrangement with Doubleday Books for Young Readers
Printed in the United States of America
April 1997
10 9 8 7 6 5 4 3 2

For my mother
H.A.
And mine, too
J.M.

Once upon a time there was an old man who lived alone with his three old pets. There was his dog, Peppy, who was very old. There was his cat, Ginger, who was very, very old. And there was Lightning, his tropical fish, who was so old that she could barely swim and preferred to float.

One day the Old Man called his three pets together and said to them, "The trouble, my friends, is that we are all so very old." Peppy wagged his tail in agreement, but just barely; Ginger twitched her ears in agreement, but just barely; and Lightning waved her fin but fell over backward because of the effort involved.

"What we need," the Old Man continued, "is a charming companion—someone to take care of us and pep us up." Lightning and Ginger and Peppy thought the Old Man was right. But this time they were too tired to wag, twitch, or wave in agreement.

That very day the Old Man put an ad in the newspaper. The ad said:

Wanted: A charming companion.
[Signed] The Old Man.

Early the next morning a furry stranger knocked on the Old Man's door. He had long white teeth and long black nails. Handing the old man an engraved visiting card, he introduced himself.

"Cuthbert Q. Devine, at your service," he said, tipping his hat. "Did you advertise for a charming companion, Old Man?"

"Yes, I did," the Old Man said.

"Look no further! I am the very one you have been searching for." Cuthbert smiled from ear to ear. "Many people think that I am a wolf. That, of course, is nonsense, utter nonsense. As a matter of fact, I happen to be a dog—a German shepherd to be exact." And Cuthbert laughed in a deep, wolfish voice.

The Old Man was completely dazzled by Cuthbert Q. Devine's charming personality. He particularly liked his bright smile. And because the Old Man's eyesight was not what it used to be, he did not see Cuthbert for what he really was—a wolf!

"You are hired," the Old Man said. And Cuthbert Q. Devine moved in, bag and baggage.

Cuthbert had not been on the job twenty-four hours before the Old Man and his three pets wondered how they had ever managed without him. First up and last to bed, Cuthbert cleaned and cooked and paid the bills. He took Peppy for long walks. He groomed Ginger and introduced her to the use of catnip. He fixed up Lightning's aquarium. He was a whiz at making fancy desserts.

He massaged the Old Man's toes. He played the viola. And every Saturday night he organized a fancy costume party.

If the Old Man had ever had any doubts about Cuthbert, they were all gone now. Cuthbert had a heart of gold. All he wanted to do was to make the Old Man and his three pets happy.

But it was all too good to last.

Late one afternoon, after Cuthbert had tucked him into his easy chair and handed him his paper, the Old Man read a terrible thing right on page one: "Wanted for Bank Robbery," the headline said. There was a picture of a wolf in a prison uniform. It was Cuthbert! The Old Man could not believe his eyes.

"To think I hired him as a charming companion and he was a wolf the whole time!" The Old Man could not get over it. He was hurt . . . and frightened too.

Pale and shaking, the Old Man confronted Cuthbert in the kitchen. He waved the newspaper in Cuthbert's face. "And you told me you were a German shepherd," he said.

Cuthbert's spoon clattered to the kitchen floor.

"I'm no good," he sobbed. "No good at all. But I can't help it—I've never had a chance. I always wanted to be good, but everyone expected me to be bad because I'm a wolf."

And before the Old Man could say another word, Cuthbert fainted dead away.

Somehow Ginger and Peppy and the Old Man managed to drag Cuthbert to his bed. When the doctor arrived he said that Cuthbert had had a bad attack of nerves and would have to stay in bed for months if he was ever to get well again. "You've got a very sick wolf on your hands," the doctor told the Old Man as he left.

Now it was the Old Man who got up early to clean and cook and pay the bills. But he did not mind at all—in fact he felt years younger. Peppy helped; so did Ginger.

With so much to do for Cuthbert, Peppy forgot his aches and pains; and everyone said that Ginger was as frisky as a kitten again. Lightning did her share too: She spent her days blowing beautiful bubbles to amuse Cuthbert—it seemed to soothe his frayed nerves.

Cuthbert had to stay in bed for a long time, but at last he was well enough to get up. One day he told the Old Man how ashamed he was of robbing all those banks. He asked the Old Man what he should do.

On the Old Man's advice, Cuthbert turned himself in to the police. When his case came to court, Cuthbert promised the judge that he would never rob a bank again. The judge believed him and said, "I will let you go this time because you have done so much for the Old Man and his pets."

The Old Man was very happy. So was Cuthbert, but his paws shook from relief.

Cuthbert finally got completely well and lived with the Old Man and his three pets for the rest of their lives. As a matter of fact, all five of them are still living in Arizona to this day. The Old Man moved there with Lightning and Ginger and Peppy because the desert climate was better for Cuthbert's health.